I'm a Frog!
By Mo Willems

Ribbit!

Ribbit!
Ribbit!
Ribbit!
Ribbit!
Ribbit!

To Trixie,
and her abundant imagination

ISBN 978-1-338-21368-3

12 11 10 9 8 7 6 5 4 3 2 17 18 19 20 21 22

Printed in the U.S.A. 40

First Scholastic printing, September 2017

I'm a Frog!

Ribbit!
Ribbit!
Ribbit!
Ribbit!

Ribbit!

Piggie?

Ribbit!
Ribbit!
Ribbit!

Ribbit!
Ribbit!

What are you doing, Piggie?

I'm a frog.

You are a . . . frog?
Yes!

I did not know that.

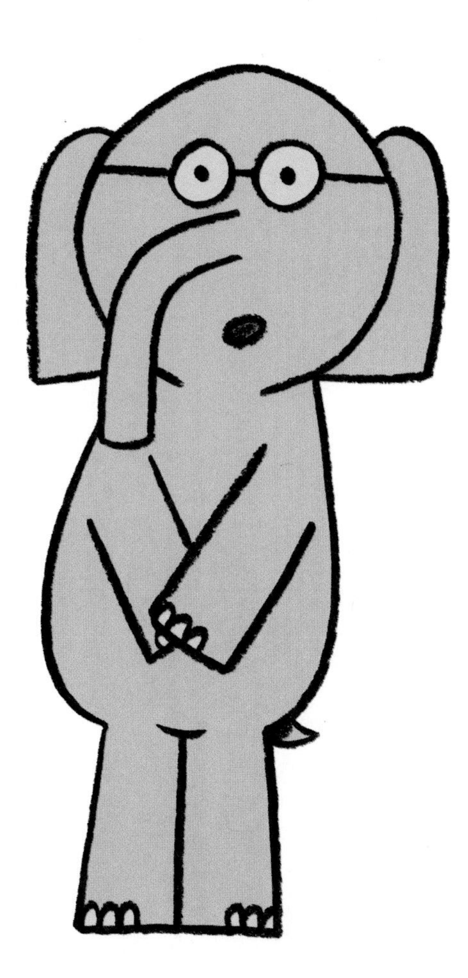

I was sure you were a pig.

You look like a pig.

And your name *is* "Piggie."

I *was* a pig.
Now I am a frog.

Ribbit!

You learn something new every day!

When did you
become a frog?

About five minutes ago.

FIVE MINUTES AGO!?!

FIVE MINUTES AGO SHE WAS A PIG!

NOW SHE IS
A FROG!

Ribbit!

What if *I*
become a frog?

Hopping
all day…

Eating
flies!

Ribbit!

I DO NOT
TO BE A

WANT FROG!!!

It is okay,
Gerald.

It is pretend.

IT IS *THE END*!?!

No, Gerald.
Pre-tend.

I am
pretending.

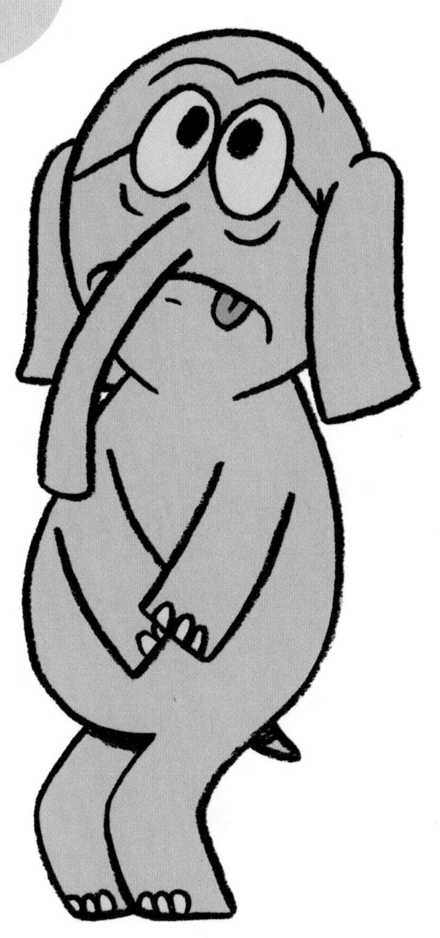

What is
“pre-tend-ing”?

Pretending is when you
act like something
you are not.

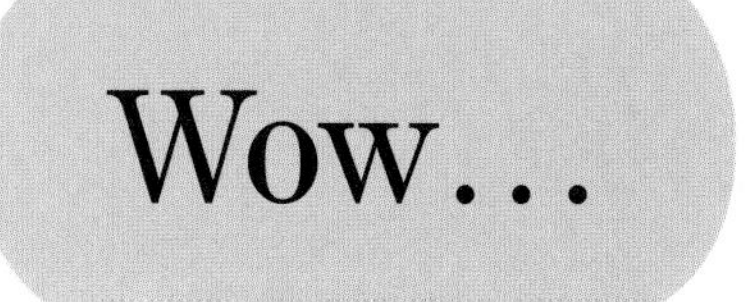
Wow…

And you can just *do* that?!

You can just go out and *pretend* to be something you are not!?

Sure.
Everyone
pretends.

Even grown-up people?

All the time.

You really do
learn something new
every day.

Do you want
to try it, Gerald?

Do you want
to pretend to be
a frog?

Ribbit!

I cannot.

Yes, you can.
Ribbit!

No, I can't.

Yes, you can!

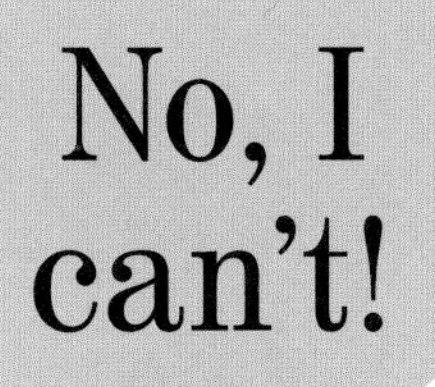

Yes, you can!

No, I can't!

No, I can't!

No, I can't!

Yes, you can!

No, I can't!

Yes, you can!

Yes, you can!
No, I can't!
Yes, you can!
Yes, you can!
No, I can't!
Yes, you can!
No! I! CAN'T!

GERALD!

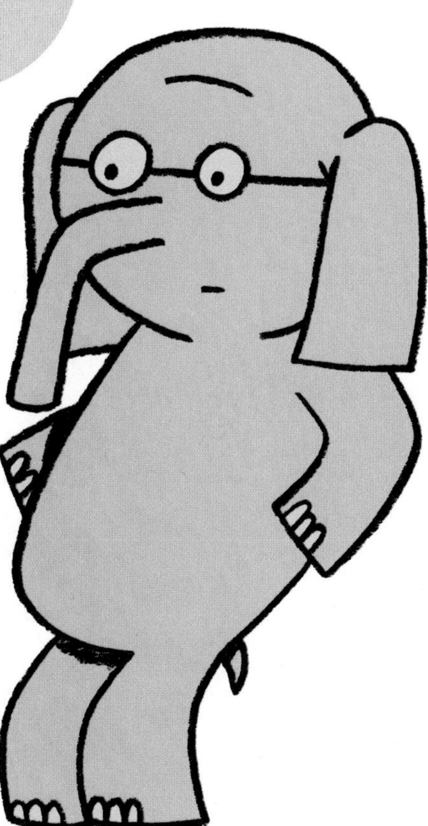

Why can't you
pretend to be
a frog!?

Because I am a cow.

Moooooooooooo!

Ribbit!
Ribbit!
Ribbit!

End!

Have you read all of Elephant and Piggie's funny adventures?

Today I Will Fly!

My Friend Is Sad

I Am Invited to a Party!

There Is a Bird on Your Head!
(Theodor Seuss Geisel Medal)

I Love My New Toy!

I Will Surprise My Friend!

Are You Ready to Play Outside?
(Theodor Seuss Geisel Medal)

Watch Me Throw the Ball!

Elephants Cannot Dance!

Pigs Make Me Sneeze!

I Am Going!

Can I Play Too?

We Are in a Book!
(Theodor Seuss Geisel Honor)

I Broke My Trunk!
(Theodor Seuss Geisel Honor)

Should I Share My Ice Cream?

Happy Pig Day!

Listen to My Trumpet!

Let's Go for a Drive!
(Theodor Seuss Geisel Honor)

A Big Guy Took My Ball!
(Theodor Seuss Geisel Honor)

I'm a Frog!

My New Friend Is So Fun!

Waiting Is Not Easy!
(Theodor Seuss Geisel Honor)

I Will Take a Nap!

I *Really* Like Slop!

The Thank You Book

Ribbit!
Moo!
Ribbit!
Woof!
Ribbit!